THE HISTORY OF POP

Ben Hubbard

🌳 Crabtree Publishing Company

www.crabtreebooks.com

Crabtree Publishing Company

www.crabtreebooks.com   1-800-387-7650
Copyright © **2009 CRABTREE PUBLISHING COMPANY**.

**Published
in Canada
Crabtree Publishing**
616 Welland Ave.
St. Catharines, ON
L2M 5V6

**Published in the
United States
Crabtree Publishing**
PMB16A
350 Fifth Ave., Suite 3308
New York, NY 10118

Content development by Shakespeare Squared
www.ShakespeareSquared.com

Author: Ben Hubbard
Project editor: Ruth Owen
Project designer: Simon Fenn
Photo research: Ruth Owen
Project coordinator: Robert Walker
Production coordinator: Katherine Berti
Prepress technicians: Samara Parent,
    Katherine Berti, Ken Wright

With thanks to
Aggie, pop advisor
extraordinaire.

Thank you to
Lorraine Petersen
and the members
of nasen

Picture credits:
Corbis: Reuters: p. 24
Getty Images: p. 5, 13 (left), 28–29; Michael Ochs Archives:
    p. 8–9, 12, 14, 15
Redferns: Richard Aaron: p. 17; Henrietta Butler: p. 22;
    Fotex: p. 31; GAB Archives: p. 13, 16; Ron Howard:
    p. 10; JM Enternational: p. 23; Hayley Madden: p. 25;
    Gilles Petard Collection: p. 11; Stefan M Prager: p. 26;
    Lex Van Rossen: p. 27
Rex Features: Orion/Everett: p. 18; Skyline Features: p. 20–21
Shutterstock: front cover, p. 1, 2–3, 4, 5 (bottom), 6–7
    (background), 14 (background), 16 (background)
WireImage: p. 6, 7, 19

Every effort has been made to trace copyright holders, and we apologize in
advance for any omissions. We would be pleased to insert the appropriate
acknowledgments in any subsequent edition of this publication.

Library and Archives Canada Cataloguing in Publication

Hubbard, Ben
    History of pop / Ben Hubbard.

(Crabtree contact)
Includes index.
ISBN 978-0-7787-3822-0 (bound).--ISBN 978-0-7787-3843-5 (pbk.)

    1. Popular music--History and criticism--Juvenile literature.
I. Title. II. Series: Crabtree contact

ML3470.H875 2009   j781.6409   C2008-907893-4

Library of Congress Cataloging-in-Publication Data

Hubbard, Ben.
    History of pop / Ben Hubbard.
        p. cm. -- (Crabtree contact)
    Includes index.
    ISBN 978-0-7787-3843-5 (pbk. : alk. paper) -- ISBN
978-0-7787-3822-0 (reinforced library binding : alk. paper)
    1. Popular music--History and criticism--Juvenile literature.
I. Title. II. Series.

    ML3470.H83 2009
    781.640973--dc22

                                2008052417

CONT

CHAPTER 1 WHAT IS POP MUSIC?

Have you ever found yourself humming and tapping along to the radio?

At the **chorus**, did you break suddenly and loudly into song?

Did the tune go around and around in your head for the rest of the day?

That's pop music!

Pop is short for popular music.

All pop songs have the same things in common.

- A "hook" (some words or a tune) that you remember.
- **Verses** and choruses
- The song is 2 1/2 to 5 1/2 minutes long.
- Guitars, bass, drums, keyboards, and singing
- The song is released as a single and bought mainly by young people.
- If enough people buy the song, it will make it onto the music charts.

Music fans listen to the latest pop songs in a 1950s record shop.

The music charts tell us which artist sold the most singles in a week.

Every pop star wants his or her song to reach "Number 1." The star also wants it to stay at Number 1 for a long time!

*Justin Timberlake wins the best pop vocal performance and best pop vocal album at the 2004 **Grammy awards**.*

Success in the charts can make singers and band members rich and famous.

Record companies earn millions of dollars from their top stars.

And the fans?

Millions of pop fans all over the world buy records and dream of meeting their idols!

Jennifer Lopez meets fans at an awards ceremony

CHAPTER 2

THE EARLY YEARS

Pop music was born in the 1950s.
This happened for two reasons.
In the 1950s, the music charts began
and rock and roll was invented!

Rock and roll was a blend of **blues** music
and **country** music.

Singers and bands performed the songs.
But older songwriters wrote the songs.

Pop music grew out of 1950s rock and roll.

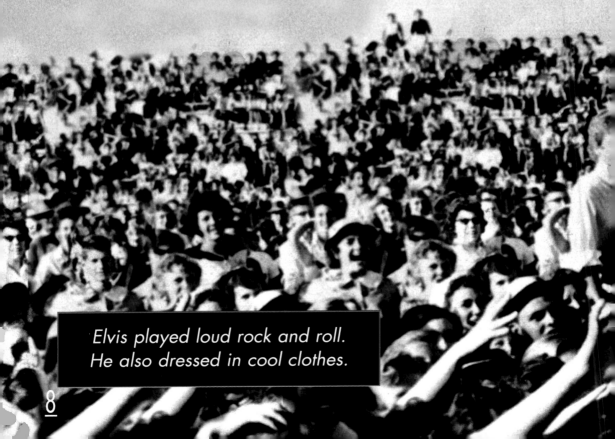

*Elvis played loud rock and roll.
He also dressed in cool clothes.*

Elvis Presley was the world's first pop star.

His singing and dancing offended parents everywhere. But teenagers loved him!

Elvis had 18 Number 1 hits. He spent 80 weeks at the top of the charts. He is one of the most popular artists in music history.

In the 1960s, young bands began writing their own songs.

In Britain, The Beatles wrote one hit after another.

Their young fans could not buy the records fast enough!

The Beatles had many Number 1 hits in Britain and the U.S. Their song, *Yesterday,* has been recorded over 3,000 times by different artists.

It is said that The Beatles have sold over one billion albums. This makes them the best-selling band of all time.

In the US, the Motown label was set up to record mainly African-American artists.

Groups such as The Jackson 5, The Temptations, and The Supremes created the "Motown sound." It was a mixture of **soul**, **funk**, blues, and **gospel**.

The Supremes had a run of Number 1 hits in the 1960s. These included *Baby Love* and *Stop! In the Name of Love.*

The Supremes

CHAPTER 3

THE 1970s

In the 1970s, a new glittering pop scene took over from rock and roll.

In the US, artists such as Stevie Wonder and Marvin Gaye made sure the Motown sound stayed alive and well in pop music.

In the UK, artists such as David Bowie and Elton John went glam rock! They wore shiny suits and platform boots.

These artists were both singers and songwriters.

David Bowie

Then came disco!

Disco was born from the funk, soul, and **Latin music** played in US nightclubs.

ABBA and the Bee Gees shared the disco throne. They created night fever and dancing queens everywhere!

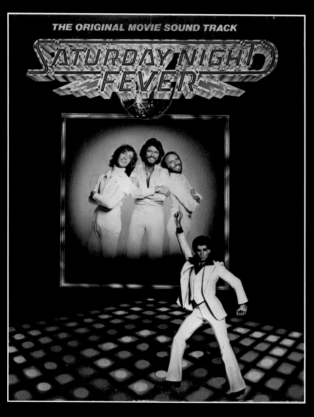

In 1977, the disco movie *Saturday Night Fever* was released. The Bee Gees wrote and performed most of the songs on the soundtrack.

ABBA

13

1970s POP PROFILE
ELTON JOHN

- 59 top 40 singles
- Seven Number 1 albums

Elton John's best-selling single is *Candle in the Wind 1997.* It was recorded in 1997 to honor Diana, Princess of Wales. It sold 37 million copies.

nigel

 I always liked spending my money. Even when I was a kid, when I had a paper round.

Elton John

1970s POP PROFILE
STEVIE WONDER

- Over 30 top ten singles
- 12 top ten albums

Stevie Wonder became blind just hours after he was born. By the time he was 11, he was already a pop star.

 Just because a man lacks the use of his eyes it doesn't mean he lacks **vision**. 🙥

Stevie Wonder

CHAPTER 4

THE 1980s

In August 1981, MTV (Music Television) was launched. Now, every new pop single had to have its own music video.

The "look" of a band was as important as their music.

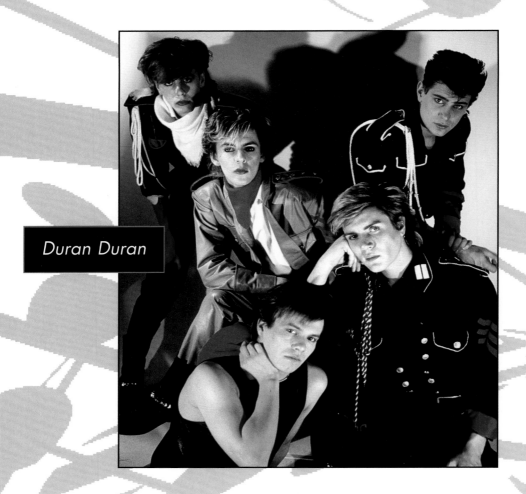

Duran Duran

Duran Duran were one of the "New Romantics" bands. These artists wore frilly shirts, "quiff" hairstyles, and eyeliner. They played moody music with good melodies.

Pop songs appeared in TV shows, movies, and even in TV ads. Songs were used to sell everything from leg warmers to toys.

Pop bands started to use new equipment. The new machines could produce thousands of different sounds all from a small keyboard device.

Prince became a huge star in the 1980s. He combined **R&B**, soul, funk, rock, jazz, and **hip hop** to create his own pop music.

Prince starred in and wrote the music for the movie Purple Rain.

1980s POP PROFILE
MADONNA

- 150 million singles sold
- 250 million albums sold

Madonna had a single in the top 40 every year from 1983 to 2004 (except for 1988 when she didn't release any singles).

In 1985, Madonna co-starred in the movie *Desperately Seeking Susan*. The movie featured Madonna's song *Into the Groove*.

Madonna (right) in Desperately Seeking Susan

> " I have the same goal I've had ever since I was a girl. I want to rule the world. "
>
> *Madonna*

Madonna is the best-selling female artist of all time. Here, she performs on stage in 2005.

1980s POP PROFILE
MICHAEL JACKSON

- 13 Number 1 singles
- 9 Number 1 hits in the 1980s
- 750 million records sold

Michael Jackson's *Thriller* is the best-selling album ever. It sold over 100 million copies.

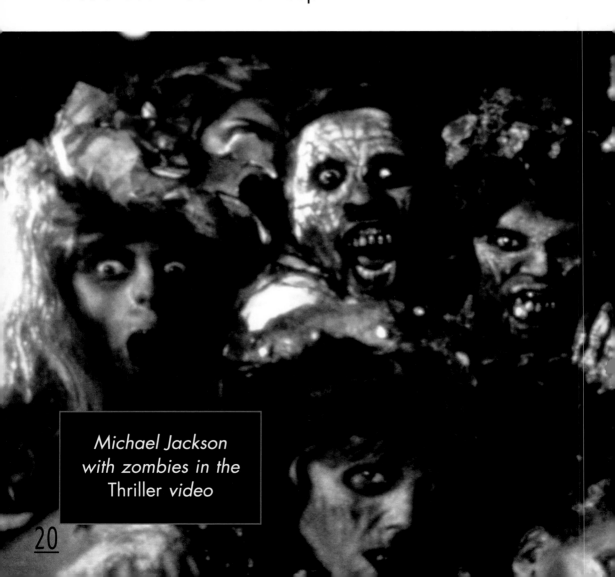

Michael Jackson with zombies in the Thriller *video*

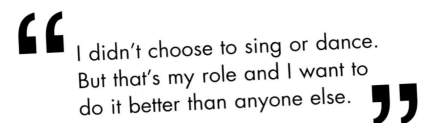 I didn't choose to sing or dance.
But that's my role and I want to
do it better than anyone else.

Michael Jackson

The music video for the single *Thriller* was 14 minutes long. It had a horror movie storyline. The video changed pop music forever. From that point on, the video was just as important as the song!

CHAPTER 5 THE 1990s

In the 1990s, manufactured pop
stole the show!

Record producers created manufactured groups.
The producers put together groups of young, good-looking
performers. They gave the groups catchy songs to sing.

The plan was to create groups who would become
enormously famous and earn millions.

The plan worked!

Boy bands ruled manufactured pop.

Groups such as Backstreet Boys, Take That,
and *NSYNC delighted fans with their catchy
vocals and well-rehearsed dance moves.

Baby Spice

Scary Spice

Sporty Spice

Posh Spice

Ginger Spice

The Spice Girls were a manufactured pop group.

Some people said the Spice Girls couldn't sing or dance. The group's fans did not agree!

The Spice Girls only recorded three albums. However, they have sold 55 million records worldwide

1990s POP PROFILE
BRITNEY SPEARS

- 83 million records sold
- 800 awards won

Britney Spears was one of the biggest pop stars in the 1990s.

Britney's album *Baby One More Time* sold over 25 million copies worldwide. It was the best-selling album ever by a teenage solo artist.

 I want to be an artist that everyone can relate to, that's young, happy, and fun.

Britney Spears

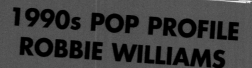

1990s POP PROFILE
ROBBIE WILLIAMS

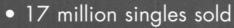

- 17 million singles sold
- 55 million albums sold

Robbie Williams was a member of the boy band *Take That*. He left the band in 1995, but he continued to sing alone.

In 2006, Robbie set a Guinness World Record when he sold 1.6 million tickets for his world tour in one day.

" I'm quite obviously not the world's most handsome man — I'm the second world's most handsome man! "

Robbie Williams

CHAPTER 6

THE 2000s

The 2000s belong to the pop **divas**!

Glamorous, talented singers such as Jennifer Lopez, Christina Aguilera, and Beyoncé have all become huge superstars.

Christina Aguilera

Christina Aguilera has sold over 42 million albums worldwide. She has also won four Grammy awards.

In the 1980s, Kylie Minogue starred in the Australian soap opera, *Neighbours*. She moved to the UK to record the song *I should be so lucky*. She became a huge pop star.

In the 2000s, Kylie is still wowing pop fans with new songs, glittering outfits, glossy videos, and glamorous concerts.

Kylie has sold over 60 million records.

Kylie Minogue

In the 2000s technology has changed pop music.

Today, we download songs from the Internet. We listen to them on computers, cell phones, and MP3 players.

Many pop stars get their starts on reality TV shows. Singers perform on live TV shows. Then millions of viewers vote for their favorite artists by text or phone.

Shows such as *Pop Idol*, *American Idol*, and *The X Factor* have produced pop stars such as Will Young, Kelly Clarkson, and Leona Lewis.

Leona Lewis won the British TV show *The X Factor* in 2006.

Leona's first single, *A Moment Like This*, broke a world record. It was downloaded over 50,000 times 30 minutes after it was released.

NEED-TO-KNOW WORDS

blues A style of sad-sounding music. It came from the songs sung by African-American slaves and farm workers

chorus The part of a song repeated after each verse

country A simple style of music played on banjos, violins, and guitars. It is often thought of as "cowboy music"

diva This word was once used to describe popular female opera singers. Today, it is often used to describe all famous female singers

funk A style of popular dance music. It has strong, rhythmic backing on bass guitar and drums

gospel American religious music based on folk music melodies mixed with elements of jazz

Grammy awards Music awards given every year

Hip-Hop A style of music with rap lyrics played over electronic music

Latin music A style of rhythmic dance music from South and Central America, Spain, and Portugal

R&B (Rhythm and Blues) Rhythm and blues is a combination of blues, soul, gospel, and jazz music. It was invented by African-American musicians in the 1940s. R&B in the 2000s features dance, disco, Hip-Hop, and soul music

record producer A person who works with music artists in a recording studio to help them create their music

soul A music style that combined the gospel music heard in African-American churches with rhythm and blues

verse Groups of lines that with a chorus form the words of a song

vision The ability to plan the future with imagination or wisdom

MORE POP FACTS

- In 2002, Elvis made a comeback—even though he died in 1977. He scored a Number 1 hit when his song *A Little Less Conversation* was updated with a modern sound and re-released.

- The Beatles had more Number 1 hits than any other band. They could have had more. However, they were often competing with their own song that was already at Number 1.

ABBA

- ABBA have sold over 400 million records worldwide. They still sell up to 4 million albums every year—even though they split up in 1982.

POP MUSIC ONLINE

www.billboard.com/
A music magazine for pop fans

www.mtv.com/
A website featuring MTV news, shows, and music videos

www.bbc.co.uk/music/
An information website about music from around the world

INDEX

Printed in the U.S.A. - BG